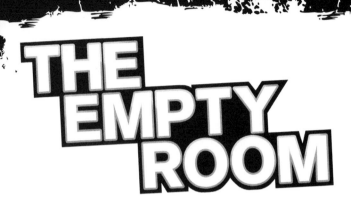

THE EMPTY ROOM

by Jon Mikkelsen
illustrated by Nathan Lueth

Librarian Reviewer
Marci Peschke
Librarian, Dallas Independent School District
MA Education Reading Specialist, Stephen F. Austin State University
Learning Resources Endorsement, Texas Women's University

Reading Consultant
Elizabeth Stedem
Educator/Consultant, Colorado Springs, CO
MA in Elementary Education, University of Denver, CO

STONE ARCH BOOKS
www.stonearchbooks.com

Keystone Books are published by Stone Arch Books
151 Good Counsel Drive, P.O. Box 669
Mankato, Minnesota 56002
www.stonearchbooks.com

Library of Congress Cataloging-in-Publication Data
Mikkelsen, Jon.
  The Empty Room / by Jon Mikkelsen; illustrated by Nathan Lueth.
  p. cm. — (Keystone Books. We Are Heroes)
  Summary: When he and his family help finish a Habitat for
Humanity house, Connor expects to be bored, but when another boy is
assigned to help him paint a bedroom, the results are surprising.
  ISBN 978-1-4342-0791-3 (library binding)
  ISBN 978-1-4342-0887-3 (pbk.)
  [1. House painting—Fiction. 2. Voluntarism—Fiction. 3. Habitat for
Humanity International, Inc.—Fiction.] I. Lueth, Nathan, ill. II. Title.
PZ7.M59268Emp 2009
[Fic]—dc22   2008008117

Art Director: Heather Kindseth
Graphic Designer: Brann Garvey

1 2 3 4 5 6 13 12 11 10 09 08

TABLE OF CONTENTS

Chapter 1

Connor Lander's dad was up to something. He'd been saying weird things for weeks. He kept dropping hints that the family was going to go somewhere. So when Connor walked into the living room, he didn't think twice about the big smile on his dad's face.

"It's going to be so great," Connor's dad said. "You guys are going to have a blast!"

"I'm sure we will," Connor replied. "So, what are we going to do?"

"You'll see," Dad said, giving Connor a wink.

Shayla, Connor's sister, came out of her room and sat down on the couch. "Is Dad still talking about the surprise?" she asked.

"Yep," Connor replied. "Just like every day."

"I bet it's a fancy vacation," Shayla said. "Or we're buying a new car."

Dad just smiled again and said, "You'll see."

Connor wandered into the kitchen. His mom was unpacking groceries. Connor started to help her.

"Mom," Connor asked, "what's the big secret? Dad makes it sound like it'll be the best thing ever."

"You know how your dad is," said Mom. "He likes things to be a surprise. He'd be upset if I told you."

Shayla walked in. She began to help Mom unpack the bags.

"Can't you give us a hint?" Shayla asked.

Mom smiled. "Let's just say it'll build character," she told them.

Connor and Shayla looked at each other nervously. If their mom said something would build character, it was not going to be any fun.

Dad walked into the kitchen. He was wearing his winter coat and a thick, warm hat. "It's time for us to get going," he said. "Get dressed, everyone. You'll need to stay warm."

Connor put on a heavy sweater. Then he pulled on his winter coat, scarf, and hat.

Everyone piled into the car. Dad drove to a part of town Connor had never seen before. There were new houses being built on the block. Almost all of them were unfinished. Dad parked the car in front of a house that looked like it was nearly done.

"Where are we?" Connor asked.

"This is our family project," said Dad. "We're going to build a house!"

Chapter 2

"We're going to build a what?" asked Connor.

"Your father is exaggerating," said Mom. "We're not building the house. It's mostly built already. We're going to help finish building this house."

Dad opened the car door and stepped out into the cold winter air. He clapped his hands together. "Let's go!" he said.

Connor and Shayla followed their parents into the house. Inside, all kinds of people were working. Some were putting up walls, some were on ladders installing lights, and some were pounding or drilling. It was so cold in the house that Connor could see his own breath.

A woman with long brown hair and a hard hat came over to them. "Welcome to Habitat for Humanity," she said, smiling. "You must be the Lander family. I'm so glad you're here to help. My name is Reba. I'm the leader of this job."

"What's Habitat for Humanity?" asked Shayla. "Is it like that makeover show on TV?"

Reba smiled. "Sort of," she said. "It's an organization that builds homes for people who need them. We ask for volunteers like you to help us construct the houses."

"That's why we're here," said Dad. "To help put the finishing touches on this house."

"Cool!" said Connor. "Do I get to use power tools or something?"

Reba laughed. "Not quite," she said. "Let's get started. Here are some helmets and safety glasses for all of you. Mrs. Lander and Shayla, you can join Mr. Givens out back to help with the deck. Mr. Lander, would you mind cutting and laying the tiles in the bathroom?"

"No problem!" Dad said.

"What do I get to do?" asked Connor. "Smash a wall with a sledgehammer? Nail some two by fours with a nail gun?"

"Actually, we were hoping you would paint one of the bedrooms," Reba said, handing him a paintbrush.

Connor groaned. He said, "Painting sounds boring and dumb. I want to use power tools!"

"Connor, all of the jobs we're doing are important," Mom said.

Shayla stuck her tongue out. Then she said, "Yeah, Connor! Now go to your room!"

Chapter 3

Reba led Connor down the hall to a bedroom. Two cans of paint sat on the floor. The paint was white. There wasn't a more boring color in the whole world. Connor knew he was going to hate his job.

"Make sure you get the paint all the way up to the ceiling," Reba said. "There's a ladder in the hallway if you need to use one."

Reba left. Connor looked around the room. The floors were still unfinished, but the room looked pretty big. Connor thought that he wouldn't mind having the room himself. It seemed like a nice room.

He started painting on the left side of the room, by the closet. At first, he made a lot of mistakes. He didn't stir the paint and it went on too thick. Then it was too thin. Then he spilled some on the floor.

After a while, Connor started to enjoy himself. He just turned up his MP3 player and painted.

An hour later, he stepped back to see how his paint job looked. He had only painted half of one of the walls.

It was going to take forever to finish the whole room!

Just then, Reba came back in the room. A kid who looked like he was Connor's age walked in behind her.

"It looks great in here, Connor!" Reba said. "I have some help for you. This is Max."

"Hi, Max," said Connor.

"Hey," Max replied. He just kept staring at the ground.

Great, Connor thought. The job was boring, the paint was boring, and now his helper was boring, too.

"I'll leave you to get to work," Reba said as she looked around the room. "You have a lot to do."

After she left, Connor handed Max a paintbrush.

"Here you go," Connor said.

"Whatever," said Max.

Connor knew it was going to be a long day.

Chapter 4

They painted in silence for twenty minutes. Finally, Connor couldn't take it anymore. He decided to try to talk to Max.

"So, where do you go to school?" Connor asked. "I haven't seen you at Armstrong Middle School."

Max didn't even look up from his paintbrush. "I don't go there," he said.

"Oh," said Connor. Another silent minute went by. "So where do you go?" Connor asked.

Max sighed. Then he said, "I go to Lincoln Middle School. It's down the street from here."

Connor could tell that Max didn't want to talk. He didn't ask any more questions.

Soon, Connor finished his wall. He needed to move to the next wall. He picked up the paintbrush and a paint can. Then he walked to the other side of the room.

As he was setting the can down, it slipped from his hands and hit the floor. Paint splashed out of the can and hit him in the face. Max laughed.

"That wasn't funny," said Connor, wiping paint off his nose.

"Yeah it was," Max said.

Connor flicked some paint at Max. A white blob of paint exploded on Max's shoulder.

"Hey!" said Max.

"I guess you're right," Connor said, smiling. "It is pretty funny."

Connor flicked a little more paint at Max. Max ducked and flung some back at Connor. Some of the paint hit Connor on the leg, but the rest landed on the wall behind him.

Connor reached into the can and scooped up paint. Then he ran at Max.

"Here it comes!" Connor yelled.

Max tried to get out of the way, but he couldn't. Connor wiped paint in Max's hair. Max laughed. Then he ran his paintbrush across Connor's face.

Connor dumped the entire paint can on Max. At the same time, Max dumped his can on Connor.

Just then, Reba flung the door open. "What is going on in here?" she yelled.

Chapter 5

MY ROOM

Reba looked shocked. "What have you two been doing?" she asked. She looked around the paint-covered room.

"It was all my fault," Max said, trying not to laugh. "I hit Connor with some paint and he threw some back."

"This room is a mess," said Reba. "We need you two to help finish this house, not tear it apart! Now clean up this mess and finish this paint job!"

Reba left the room. She shut the door loudly behind her.

When they were sure it was safe, both boys looked at each other. Then they burst out laughing.

"Wow, she was really mad," said Max. "She looked like her head was going to explode!"

"I know," said Connor. "I thought that look she gave us would take the paint off the walls by itself. But why did you take the blame? I was the one who hit you first with the paint."

Max shrugged. He said, "I figured Reba wouldn't get mad at me."

"Why not?" Connor asked, frowning.

"Because it's my house," Max said.

"What? I thought it was going to a poor family," said Connor.

Max looked at the ground. Then he said, "My dad got laid off last year and my mom is too sick to work. We moved into a shelter for a couple of months. Then Habitat for Humanity offered to help us with this house."

Max and Connor were quiet for a while. Then Max said, "It's really cool that people like you will volunteer to help out people who need it."

"I almost didn't want to come here today," said Connor. "I thought it was going to be boring and dumb. But painting is kind of fun. And it was cool to meet you."

Max smiled. Then he looked around at the mess. "I guess we should start cleaning up my room," he said.

"This is your room?" Connor asked. "Now I do feel bad about the mess."

"Don't worry about it," said Max. "Every time I look at the walls, I'll remember what a great time we had today."

Max and Connor cleaned up the floor and re-painted the walls. By the time they were done, it was impossible to tell they had made such a mess.

In one corner of the room, they lifted the plastic sheet off the floor. Then they each dipped a hand in the leftover paint and made a handprint on the wood floor.

"It's sort of like how a painter signs his name on his paintings," Connor said.

"Cool!" Max said.

They went out to the front of the house to join the rest of the volunteers.

"Where are you staying until your house is done?" asked Connor.

"We're just staying a few more nights at the shelter," Max told him.

Connor thought for a minute. Then he said, "Maybe you could stay with us for a day or so. I think my room could use a new coat of paint. And we already proved we're the best painters in town!"

33

ABOUT THE AUTHOR

Jon Mikkelsen has written dozens of plays for kids, which have involved aliens, superheroes, and more aliens. He acts on stage and loves performing in front of an audience. Jon also loves sushi, cheeseburgers, and pizza. He loves to travel, and has visited Moscow, Berlin, London, and Amsterdam. He lives in Minneapolis and has a cat named Coco, who does not pay rent.

ABOUT THE ILLUSTRATOR

Nathan Lueth has been a freelance illustrator since 2004. He graduated from the Minneapolis College of Art and Design in 2004, and has done work for companies like Target, General Mills, and Wreked Records. Nathan was a 2008 finalist in Tokyopop's Rising Stars of Manga contest. He lives in Minneapolis, Minnesota.

GLOSSARY

blame (BLAYM)—to say something is someone else's fault

character (KAIR-ik-tur)—if something builds character, it makes you a better person

construct (kuhn-STRUCKT)—to build

exaggerating (eg-ZAJ-uh-rayt-ing)—making something seem bigger, better, or more important than it is

hints (HINTS)—clues or helpful tips

impossible (im-POSS-uh-buhl)—if something is impossible, it is unable to be done or cannot be true

installing (in-STAWL-ing)—putting something in place, ready to be used

organization (or-guh-nuh-ZAY-shuhn)—a number of people working together

project (PROJ-ekt)—something being worked on

shelter (SHEL-tur)—a place where a homeless person can stay

unfinished (uhn-FIN-ishd)—not done

DISCUSSION QUESTIONS

1. Do you think Connor's dad's surprise was good or bad? Why?

2. Why do you think Max didn't talk much when he first met Connor?

3. Do you think it would be fun to help build a house? What part of building a house would you want to help with?

WRITING PROMPTS

1. What would your dream house be like? Describe it. Then draw a picture of your house, and label the rooms.

2. Sometimes it can be interesting to think about a story from another person's point of view. Try writing chapter 4 from Max's point of view. What does he see and hear? What does he think about? How does he feel?

3. What do you think happens after this book ends? Write about what Max and Connor do after they're done painting Max's room.

MORE ABOUT HABITAT FOR HUMANITY

Habitat For Humanity International is a nonprofit organization that works to eliminate poverty and homelessness.

Habitat for Humanity (HFH) was founded in 1976 by a man named Millard Fuller. He and his wife, Linda, wanted to help provide more affordable housing to people with low incomes.

Since 1976, Habitat for Humanity has built more than 225,000 houses! The houses are all over the world. More than one million people in three thousand communities have been able to afford housing because of HFH.

The houses built by Habitat for Humanity are not free.

The new homeowners pay for their houses, but because HFH is a nonprofit organization, the houses are more affordable. In addition to paying their mortgage payments, the family that buys a HFH house is expected to spend hundreds of hours of their own time working on their house and on houses for other people, too. Some people just work on a few houses, and others work on many houses.

Many volunteers, all over the world, work alongside these families. Everyone works together to turn lumber, cement, and paint into a new home.

For more information on Habitat for Humanity, go to www.habitat.org.

INTERNET SITES

Do you want to know more about subjects related to this book? Or are you interested in learning about other topics? Then check out FactHound, a fun, easy way to find Internet sites.

Our investigative staff has already sniffed out great sites for you!

Here's how to use FactHound:

1. Visit *www.facthound.com*

2. Select your grade level.

3. To learn more about subjects related to this book, type in the book's ISBN number: **9781434207913**.

4. Click the **Fetch It** button.

FactHound will fetch the best Internet sites for you!